The form suddenly burst from the bog and
came into full view. It was a ghostly, glowing
bear riding a ghostly, glowing horse! And it
was galloping right toward them!

The Berenstain Bears
and the
GALLOPING GHOST

by Stan & Jan Berenstain

A BIG CHAPTER BOOK™

Random House New York

Library of Congress Cataloging-in-Publication Data
Berenstain, Stan.
The Berenstain Bears and the galloping ghost / by Stan and Jan Berenstain.
   p.   cm. — (a Big chapter book)
SUMMARY: Brother Bear learns about fear and getting back in the saddle when a ghost haunts the riding academy.
ISBN: 0-679-85815-6 (pbk.) — ISBN 0-679-95815-0 (lib. bdg.)
[1. Bears—Fiction. 2. Fear—Fiction. 3. Horsemanship—Fiction.
4. Ghosts—Fiction.] I. Berenstain, Jan. II. Title. III. Series:
Berenstain, Stan. Big chapter book.
PZ7.B4483Beff   1994
[E]—dc20   94-2772

Manufactured in the United States of America 10 9 8 7 6 5 4 3 2 1

BIG CHAPTER BOOKS is a trademark of Berenstain Enterprises, Inc.

Contents

Chapter 1
Horses and Hauntings

Like all cubs, Brother and Sister Bear had their favorite things. They had favorite foods and drinks, favorite songs and games, favorite school subjects and TV shows. They also had favorite kinds of storybooks. Sister loved horse stories. Brother couldn't get enough spooky mysteries and ghost stories.

One spring day after school, Brother and Sister were at the Bear Country Library stocking up on books for the next couple of

weeks. When they were finished finding the books they wanted, they met at the front counter to check them out.

Ms. Goodbear, the librarian, raised her eyebrows as she placed a hand on the stack of five books that Brother had chosen. "I see you're still into the adventures of the great bear detective, Grizzlock Holmes, and his faithful assistant, Dr. Bearson," she said. "Can you really read all these books in two weeks?"

"Piece o' cake," said Brother. "I love mysteries."

"Don't they give you nightmares?" asked Ms. Goodbear.

"Nah. The scarier, the better."

"What about you, Sister?" asked Ms. Goodbear.

"I like horse stories," said Sister, pushing her two books toward the librarian. Their titles were *Brown Beauty* and *Misty of Grizzlyteague*. "I think horses are the most beautiful animals in the whole world."

"Have you ever tried a mystery story?" asked Ms. Goodbear.

Sister shook her head.

"She's afraid of spooky stuff," teased Brother. "She'll *never* read a mystery for as long as she lives."

Sister frowned. "Now wait a minute," she said. "I might read one someday." Then she added, "If it's a *horse* mystery."

"You mean like *Grizzlock Holmes and the Haunted Horseman*?" asked Brother. He grinned a wicked grin and bugged his eyes out at Sister.

Sister looked frightened. "Maybe I'll skip that one," she said.

"Just foolin', Sis," said Brother with a laugh. "There's no such book."

Ms. Goodbear decided to change the subject so that Brother would stop teasing Sister. "Have you ever ridden a horse, Sister?" she asked.

"No," said Sister. "I wanted to take riding lessons at Miss Mamie's Riding Academy last year, but Mama and Papa said I was too young. But I think I'll ask them again soon. My friend Lizzy Bruin started lessons there a couple of weeks ago, and she's a whole month younger than I am."

"If I remember correctly," said Ms. Goodbear, "my daughter, Susie, started lessons with Miss Mamie when she was your age."

"That does it," said Sister. "I'll ask Mama

and Papa about lessons tomorrow."

Later that night, the cubs lay in their bunk beds in the dark bedroom, reading library books by flashlight under the covers. Now and then, Sister would take time out from reading about horses and think about riding them. Tomorrow she would be asking Papa and Mama about riding lessons.

"Hey, listen to this," Brother whispered to Sister. Sister lay *Brown Beauty* down across her chest as Brother read aloud from *Grizzlock Holmes and the Speckled Band.*

"'As Holmes lay abed in the darkened room,'" Brother read, "'all of a sudden the servants' bell-cord above the bed began to move ever so slightly. Holding his breath, Holmes peered up into the darkness.'"

Sister stared up at the blank ceiling and pulled the covers up to her chin.

Brother continued, "'As he watched, the

bell-cord grew thick with moving, twisting coils. Something was slithering down the cord *and right at his face!*' "

Sister clapped her hands over her ears and screamed, "Mama-a-a-a-a!"

Mama and Papa came bounding up the stairs. "What's the matter?" asked Mama.

"Brother scared me with his Grizzlock Holmes book!" Sister wailed.

"How?" asked Papa.

MAMA-A

"He read some of it to me," said Sister.

Brother couldn't help chuckling.

"Cut that out, Brother," ordered Papa. "Scaring your little sister isn't funny."

"But she didn't tell me not to read it...," said Brother.

"That doesn't matter one bit," said Mama. "You know that spooky stories give Sister nightmares. From now on keep them to yourself."

"Flashlights out," said Papa. "Go to sleep. Both of you."

The cubs listened as their parents' footsteps grew fainter on the stairs. The room was dark and quiet.

Brother lay still for a minute or so, staring into the darkness. Then he propped himself up on one elbow, cupped a hand over his mouth, and whispered up at Sister, *"Scaredy-bear."*

Chapter 2
Riding Lessons

The next day, Sister brought home from school a folder about Miss Mamie's Riding Academy. Lizzy Bruin had given it to her. She showed it to Papa, who was reading the afternoon paper in the living room.

"Good grief!" said Papa. "You're already into ballet, gymnastics, and soccer. Isn't that enough for one cub? And what about your schoolwork?"

"Oh, Papa," said Sister. "Horses are so wonderful. Lizzy Bruin has been taking lessons for just two weeks and she's already galloping! There's a horse named Flash that

Lizzy says is the most beautiful in Bear Country…"

Papa hadn't realized how much in love with horses his daughter was. As she went on and on about them, he examined the folder. Brother came over and looked at it over Papa's shoulder.

"I could drop swimming," said Sister eagerly. "And if the riding lessons still cost too much…"

"No, no," said Papa. "Don't you worry about the cost. You and Brother could *both* take riding lessons for the price of your swim club membership. Miss Mamie charges so little that I wonder how she manages to stay in business. I suppose it's all right for you two to take riding lessons. What do you think, Mama?"

Mama had come in from the kitchen. "I think it's a fine idea," she said.

"Hurray!" shouted Sister. "We're going to take riding lessons! Isn't that great!"

"Sure, great," mumbled Brother.

But only Mama noticed that Brother didn't seem very excited about the idea.

Chapter 3
Miss Mamie's Problem

Miss Mamie's place was outside of town in a deserted area near Forbidden Bog. It didn't look like much. The sign out front, which read MISS MAMIE'S RIDING ACADEMY, was overgrown with vines. The split-rail fence was covered with thornbushes. The buildings were weathered and worn.

Apart from a small toolshed, there were three buildings in all. The one marked OFFICE wasn't much larger than the tool-shed behind it. Another, marked STABLES, was long and low. The third was the riding arena, a huge building as big as the three barns put together.

The office door opened and out came Miss Mamie. She was big and strong-looking. She moved briskly along the path, even though she walked with a limp. She always wore the same outfit: an extra-large workshirt and double-extra-large britches that she ordered from the L. L. Bear cata-log. As she walked to the mailbox, she used her riding crop to whip at the weeds that had grown over the path. She collected the day's mail and returned to the office, where she sat in her old wooden chair behind her old wooden desk.

The desk was so cluttered with papers and bills that Miss Mamie had to clear a space whenever she wanted to work on something. The wall behind the desk was covered with framed photos. In one, a very young Miss Mamie sat on a horse in mid-leap over a fence. Another showed a still-young Miss Mamie nuzzling a horse. A third

showed an older Miss Mamie holding a winner's cup.

As she looked through her mail, one of the envelopes caught Miss Mamie's eye. She opened it and began to read. She was frowning down at it when Gus, her helper and handybear, opened the front door and walked in.

"Horses are all put away for the night, Miss Mamie," he said.

"Are *all* the stable windows locked this time?" asked Miss Mamie.

"I checked every one of 'em," said Gus. "But like I told you this morning, I wasn't the one who left that window open last night."

"So you say, Gus," said Miss Mamie. "But we can't be too careful. The nights are still chilly. If there's a next time, the horses could get sick and we'd be in trouble. I'd have to cancel lessons until they got well...and..."

"And what, Miss Mamie?" asked Gus.

"And we just can't afford to lose any money right now," said Miss Mamie. "I'm already a month behind in my mortgage payments."

Gus scratched his head and said, "Just a

month? The Great Grizzly National Bank hasn't ever bothered you about being a month or two behind. Even three."

"The bank doesn't own my mortgage anymore," said Miss Mamie. She handed Gus the letter she had been reading.

"'Property Management,'" Gus read aloud. "Hmm. Looks like these folks musta taken over your mortgage. Now that seems kinda funny, don't it? You went and borrowed money from the bank to buy this place. Now all of a sudden you're paying back a bunch of strangers instead of the bank. Supposin' I borrowed a hammer from Papa Bear, and after a while Papa came to me and said, 'Farmer Ben owns that hammer now, 'cause I sold it to him.' I'm not sure I'd like that. Farmer Ben's not a close friend of mine, and I only borrow from close friends."

"That's exactly what worries me," said Miss Mamie. "I borrowed money from the bank because I know those folks and they know me. They know I get behind sometimes on my mortgage payments. But they also know if they're patient, I'll get caught up before too long. I'm a little worried about these Property Management folks. Read it out loud, Gus."

"'We call to your attention,'" read Gus, "'that you are now one month behind on your mortgage. We trust that you will make that payment without delay.' "

"See?" said Miss Mamie. "That's why we don't want to cancel any lessons. We can't afford it."

Gus looked worried. "Do you think these folks are gonna make trouble?"

"I sure hope not," said Miss Mamie. "Because I may not be able to make that payment until the end of next month."

Property Management Inc
Bear Country

Miss Mamie
Miss Mamie's Riding Academy
Bear Country

Dear Miss Mamie:

We call to your attention that you are now one month behind on your mortgage. We trust that you will make that payment without delay.

Yours truly,

[signature]

Mortgage Officer

Chapter 4
A Morning at the Academy

After breakfast on Saturday morning, the Bear family climbed into their red roadster and drove off down the winding road toward Miss Mamie's Riding Academy. Sister was all abuzz with excitement, but Brother sat quietly looking out at the spring scenery.

After a while they drove alongside Forbidden Bog. That meant that the riding academy was only minutes away. But Brother didn't have his mind on horses or riding. Instead, he peered out into the gloom of the swamp and he thought of the famous legend of the Galloping Ghost of Forbidden Bog.

"Papa?" he asked. "How did the legend of the Galloping Ghost get started?"

"An interesting story," said Papa. "Long, long ago, there was a bear named Billy Beechtree, who suffered a terrible fate in Forbidden Bog. One day he was falsely accused of being a highwaybear—of robbing travelers along this very road. A mob

of angry citizens chased him into the bog, where he and his horse were swallowed up by a pool of quicksand. According to the legend, from time to time, the ghost of Billy Beechtree rises from his quicksand grave and gallops on his phantom horse over the countryside, crying for justice."

"Stop it, Papa," said Sister. "You're scaring me."

"Sorry, honey," said Papa. "I forgot."

"But it's just a legend," Brother told Sister. "There are no such things as ghosts."

"It still scares me," said Sister. "Even if it's just a legend." But she didn't look so sure about its being just a legend.

Soon the Bears' roadster turned down the long dirt driveway to the riding academy. No one was in sight. But as they neared the building marked OFFICE, they noticed a fellow wearing a baseball cap standing off to one side. He was watering the grass with a garden hose.

"Hey, look! It's Gus!" said Sister. "From school!"

Gus also worked part-time as the custodian of Bear Country School. Brother, who was getting more and more nervous about riding lessons, was glad to see a familiar

face at the academy.

"Hey, Gus," called Papa. "Where is everybody?"

"Well, howdy, Papa," Gus called back. He took off his cap and waved it at the riding arena. "They're all in there. There's a lesson under way right now." He turned off the hose and came over. "I'll take you folks to the office and give Miss Mamie a holler on the loudspeaker. Follow me."

Inside the arena a lot of riding was going on. Older cubs on full-size horses trotted around a large outer ring, while younger cubs rode ponies around an inner ring. The riders were watched closely by three teenage assistants who were expert riders. Meanwhile, Miss Mamie strolled back and forth from one end of the arena to the other. She kept an eye on everything. She

carried a long trainer's whip and shouted instructions through a megaphone.

A voice came over the loudspeaker. It was Gus calling Miss Mamie to the office. Miss Mamie left one of her young assistants in charge and made her way to the office. As she opened the front door, she saw Papa Bear frowning at the jumble of papers on her desk. Mama was staring at a pile of rusty old horseshoes in one corner.

"Well, if it isn't the Bear family," said Miss Mamie with a smile. "I'll bet you cubs are interested in learning to ride. Am I right?"

Sister nodded and grinned eagerly up at the riding teacher. Brother nodded too, but looked away. Miss Mamie was big and loud, and that made Brother even more nervous about riding.

"Please excuse the mess in here," Miss Mamie said to Mama and Papa. "I've never been much good at keeping the business end of things neat and tidy."

"Don't give it a second thought," said Mama. "What's most important at a riding school is safety, not neatness."

That made Miss Mamie and Gus look at

each other for a moment. They were both thinking of the stable window that had been left open two nights before. And of the hose that had been left running in the arena the night before.

For years Gus had watered down the rings for a few minutes at the end of each day. But this was the first time he had ever left the hose on, flooding the rings. He and Miss Mamie had worked hard since dawn to drain the rings and sand them down. Mamie was afraid she would have to cancel the morning's lessons. She knew she couldn't afford to lose any money if she

wanted to make that mortgage payment. Luckily, by lesson time the rings had been just dry enough for riding. Gus, of course, was sure he had turned off the hose. Miss Mamie wondered if maybe Gus wasn't becoming a little forgetful.

"I'm sure you run a safe school," said Papa. "But have you had the place checked out for ghosts lately?"

"If you're talking about the legend of the Galloping Ghost," said Miss Mamie, "I'd rather you didn't."

HAVE YOU HAD THE PLACE CHECKED OUT FOR GHOSTS LATELY?

"Me, too," said Sister with a shiver.

"Just joking," said Papa. "After all, your place is right next to Forbidden Bog."

"I don't believe in the Galloping Ghost or any other ghost, for that matter," said Miss Mamie. "But other folks do. So it's just not good business to talk about it. Say," she said, changing the subject, "did Gus show you folks around yet? No? Well, come on. I'll give you the guided tour."

Sister was excited to see her friends Lizzy Bruin, Queenie McBear, and Babs Bruno riding around the rings in the arena. She waved to them. They smiled but couldn't wave back because they were holding the reins.

The full-size horses seemed kind of scary to Brother. They were so big. He was glad he didn't have to climb up on one yet.

When the class had ended and the students and the Bear family had all gone home, Miss Mamie returned to the office. She leaned back in her chair and swung her boots up onto the desk. She smiled. Getting two new students would help her pay that mortgage sooner. If Gus will just be a little more careful, she thought, everything will be okay.

Chapter 5
Brother Takes a Spill

When Brother and Sister returned to the riding academy for their first lessons, Miss Mamie gave them a lot of attention. She watched as two of the teenage assistants helped them onto their horses. Then she gave them last-minute instructions.

"Today you're just going to walk your horses around a little," she said. "I want you to relax in the saddle and never stand on the stirrups. Hold the reins firmly, but don't pull on them unless one of my assistants or I tell you to. And don't worry—you'll do just fine."

The assistants led Brother on his horse and Sister on her pony into the rings to join the other riders. Sister was in heaven. Each time she circled the ring, she passed Flash, the beautiful horse Lizzy had told her about. Flash was tied to a railing at one end of the arena. He was resting. Whenever she passed him, Sister thought of how wonderful it would be to ride him in a few more weeks.

Brother didn't feel at all as if he were in heaven. But riding wasn't as scary as he

had thought it would be. Though he was very high off the ground, his horse seemed calm and careful. He felt relieved. Now he could relax, and his friends would never even know how nervous he had been about riding.

Just then something happened that changed everything. Flash had started to

grow restless at his end of the arena. He turned his head this way and that. He did this whenever he felt well rested and ready to return to the ring. Just as Brother was passing him, Flash gave his rope a tug that pulled the whole railing from the wall. It fell to the ground with a clatter, which made Flash rear up on his hind legs and whinny.

The clatter and whinny frightened Brother's horse. Suddenly it broke into a gallop and headed across the arena. The other horses followed.

"Rein in!" roared Miss Mamie. "Rein in!"

Sister, Queenie, Babs, and the rest quickly reined in their horses, slowing and

stopping them. But Brother panicked. He let go of the reins and lost his balance. As he fell, his foot caught in the stirrup. Luckily, an assistant dashed over, grabbed the reins, and pulled Brother's horse to a stop.

Brother wasn't really hurt. But he was very frightened and embarrassed. The assistant helped him to his feet and steadied his horse so that he could get back on.

"That's right!" called Queenie McBear. "When you take a spill, get right back on the horse!"

"Yeah!" the other students agreed.

But Brother didn't want any part of their advice. Miss Mamie could see that. After dusting him off, she walked with Brother out of the arena and down the path to the office.

Chapter 6
Brother's New Friend

Brother sat in the office with his head bowed. He was afraid that Miss Mamie would be hard on him about not getting back on the horse after his fall. The big, gruff riding teacher stood in front of him, hands on hips. He looked up sheepishly and said, "I'm sorry, Miss Mamie. I should have got back on."

"Nonsense," said Miss Mamie. "That 'get back on' stuff is a lot of bunk. What's important is that you're not hurt. How about

MIND IF I ASK YOU SOMETHING PERSONAL?

a mug of hot chocolate?"

"Sure," said Brother. "Thanks." He felt better already. Miss Mamie was still gruff and loud. But somehow she was gruff and loud in a gentle way.

Miss Mamie dug an old hot plate out of the clutter on her desk and made hot chocolate for Brother and herself. "Mind if I ask you something personal?" she asked.

"Go ahead," said Brother.

"Were you maybe just a little bit afraid of

horses even before you got thrown?"

"Maybe," Brother admitted. "A little."

"Well, there's nothing strange about that," said Miss Mamie. "Sometimes I think the cubs who *aren't* afraid of horses are the strange ones! You know, when I was a cub and started riding, I was scared to death of horses. Here's your hot chocolate." Miss Mamie looked over at the wall. It was full of championship photos and winner's cups. "But I grew up in a riding family, so I didn't have any choice but to overcome my fears."

"But you became a great rider," said Brother, sipping his hot chocolate. "A champion."

"I guess I did," said Miss Mamie. "But I'll tell you something: I was real scared at the start."

"Did you ever get thrown?" asked Brother.

"Did I ever!" said Miss Mamie. "I can't count how many times. But I never got badly hurt until that last one. It was nine years ago. I was riding in a steeplechase—that's a race with jumps. My horse landed short at a water jump. Broke my leg in two places. It didn't heal right. I guess you noticed my limp."

Brother nodded.

"Haven't been on a horse since," said Miss Mamie.

"In nine years?" said Brother. "Why not?"

Miss Mamie stared off into space for a moment. Then she looked at Brother as if she had forgotten he was there. "Scared, I guess," she said. "So, what'll it be? You gonna keep riding or call it quits? It's up to you. You don't have to take lessons just because your sister's taking them. Of course, if you want to keep going, we'll be mighty glad to have you."

Brother thought for a moment. A few minutes ago he had been scared and embarrassed. But after talking with Miss Mamie, he felt a whole lot better about riding. And he felt a lot better about Miss Mamie, too. Even though he hadn't known her long, he knew he had found a good friend. "I'll keep going," he said finally. "I think I can handle it."

"I *know* you can," said Miss Mamie. "But you just rest up right here for the time being. You can get back on that horse when your next lesson comes around."

The door opened and Gus poked his head in. "You all right, Brother?" he asked.

"Fine," said Brother.

"Glad to hear it." Gus came in and handed the mail to Miss Mamie. "I think you ought to look at this one right away, Miss Mamie," he said, pointing to the letter on top of the stack of mail. "It's from those Property Management folks."

Miss Mamie just glared at Gus. "What in tarnation happened to that railing!" she barked.

"Came clear off the wall," said Gus. "The bolts must have been loose."

"How could you let those bolts get so loose?" said Miss Mamie. "Students could have been badly hurt."

"But I didn't let them get loose, Miss Mamie," said Gus. "I check those bolts once a week like clockwork. Until today we've never had so much as a wobble from that railing."

"Well, from now on you'd better check them *twice* a week," said Miss Mamie. "What'll parents think? I'll tell you what they'll think. They'll think that this place isn't safe. That kind of accident can hurt cubs...and hurt business, too. How would I pay that mortgage on time?"

"I still think you'd better look at this," said Gus. He pointed to the letter again.

Miss Mamie opened it. As she read, her

I STILL THINK YOU'D BETTER LOOK AT THIS.

face sagged. She let out a long sigh and slumped in her chair. Finally she hauled her heavy body from the chair and limped out of the office.

Gus picked up the letter from the desk and read it. "Oh, my goodness," he said.

"What's wrong?" asked Brother.

"Plenty," said Gus. "But it's not something a cub could understand."

"Please, Gus. Tell me," said Brother. "Maybe there's some way I could help."

"I doubt it," said Gus. "But here's what's goin' on. Miss Mamie took out a mortgage to buy this place. Got it from the bank—"

Mortgage, thought Brother. What the heck is a *mortgage*?

"Well," continued Gus, "she's been in arrears lately—Mamie's a great horsebear, but she's not much of a businessbear—"

Arrears, thought Brother. What the heck is *arrears*?

"But that wasn't a problem. At least, not until these Property Management people took over the mortgage. Now they're threatening to foreclose. If she doesn't pay up in thirty days, they're gonna take her place away."

Mortgage? Arrears? Foreclose? Gus was right. It *wasn't* something a cub could understand.

But Gus was still talking. "And now we're having these danged accidents. Why, if I didn't know better, I'd say someone was trying to close Miss Mamie down—trying to

put her out of business. Dang it!"

Now it was as if Gus were talking to himself. It was as if Brother weren't even there: "Maybe this place *is* haunted!" he said. Then, with one more "Dang it!" he slammed the letter down on Miss Mamie's desk and stormed out of the office.

But of course Brother was still there. And while he couldn't quite understand everything that was going on, it sure sounded like a mystery. Just the sort of mystery Grizzlock Holmes solved in story after story.

But this wasn't a story. This was real life, with a very real Miss Mamie about to lose her riding academy.

That's when a very interesting thought came to Brother. What would Grizzlock Holmes do to solve the Case of the Haunted Riding Academy? For one thing, thought Brother, he would focus on

details—details like the letter. Then Brother did something he knew he wasn't supposed to do. He read someone else's mail.

There were those words again—and lots of others. Brother knew what Grizzlock Holmes would do if he didn't understand something. He'd talk it over with his smarter brother, Grizzcroft Holmes. Now, Brother Bear didn't have a smarter brother, but he did have a smarter *cousin*, Cousin Fred. Brother tore a piece of paper from Miss Mamie's notepad and wrote down these words: mortgage, arrears, and foreclose.

Cousin Fred, who read the dictionary for fun, would know what they meant. That would be a beginning, at least.

Chapter 7
Dictionary Fred Strikes Again

"'Mortgage,'" said Fred as he and Brother walked to school the next morning. "The transfer of property to a creditor as a security for repayment of a loan."

"Hunh?" said Brother.

Luckily, Cousin Fred knew not only the meaning of the word. He also knew something about the real-estate business. "It's like this," he told Brother. "Years ago Miss Mamie decided to buy the old run-down riding academy out by Forbidden Bog. But she didn't have enough money. So she borrowed the money from Great Grizzly National Bank. She has to pay all that money back before she really owns the property. That can take many years. Miss Mamie pays back a little bit of the loan each month—that's the mortgage."

"What's 'arrears'?" asked Brother.

"Behind on her payments," said Fred. "If that happens, the bank can *foreclose*. That means the bank takes charge of the academy and sells it to someone else."

"But the bank doesn't own Miss Mamie's mortgage," said Brother. He had suddenly remembered what Gus had told him. "Something called Property Management owns it."

"A property management company," said Fred. "Hmm, interesting. Someone must have bought Miss Mamie's mortgage from the bank and hired Property Management to handle Miss Mamie's payments. Perfectly legal." He smiled. "Is your head spinning yet?"

"Yeah," said Brother. "But I think I'm catching on. Thanks."

"Glad to be of help," said Fred.

"Listen, there's another way you can help," said Brother. "Come out to the academy with me tomorrow after school. While I'm having my riding lesson, you can sort of sniff around the place where the accidents happened. Maybe you can sniff out a few clues. If someone doesn't put a stop to these accidents, Miss Mamie is sure to lose the academy."

Cousin Fred thought that maybe Gus was just getting forgetful in his old age. But Brother seemed so sure that something else was causing the accidents. Fred agreed to help.

Chapter 8
Fear of Falling

At dinner that evening, Brother asked Papa what he thought of the mysterious accidents at the riding academy.

"So Gus swears he didn't cause them," said Papa with a chuckle. "Sounds to me like he's just making excuses for not doing his job." Papa swallowed a mouthful of grilled brook trout. He frowned. "Funny thing, though. Gus and I have been friends a long time. And I've never known him to do sloppy work."

Brother told Papa about Miss Mamie's problem with her mortgage.

"Dear me, that's awful," said Papa. "But not surprising. Miss Mamie is a great old horsebear and a terrific riding teacher. But as good a horsebear as she is, that's how bad a businessbear she is. There's no way she can make a profit from those small fees she charges. Her place is a mess. There's no insulation. Her heating bills must be enormous. By the way, I hear you had a little problem yourself at the academy. About staying on your horse?"

Brother just nodded. He didn't really want to talk about that. But Sister was still angry that he had teased her about being afraid of spooky stories.

"A *little* problem?" she said. "He sat on that horse like a sack of potatoes. Then the horse shied and he let go of the reins and fell off. You know what I think?"

A LITTLE PROBLEM? HE SAT ON THAT HORSE LIKE A SACK OF POTATOES.

"That will be enough, Sister," said Mama.

"I think he's scared," said Sister. "Just plain chicken *scared*."

"Oh, yeah!" said Brother. "Well, if I'm scared, at least I'm scared of something *real*. Not like you—scared of silly imaginary things like ghosts." He made a scary face and reached out toward Sister. "Who-o-o-o! I'm the Galloping Ghost of Forbidden Bog and I'm gonna get you-o-o-o!"

Sister let out a scream and ran into the living room.

"That's enough!" bellowed Papa. "Back to the table!"

I'M GONNA GET YOU-O-O-O

Sister came back into the dining room and sat down. She glared at her brother.

"Now listen, you two," said Papa. "It isn't fair to tease others about their fears. Because *everyone* is afraid of *something*."

"Everyone?" asked Brother.

"That's right."

"What are you afraid of, Papa?" asked Sister.

Papa grinned. "Your mama."

Mama pretended not to hear Papa's remark.

"And what are you afraid of, Mama?" asked Brother.

"What I'm afraid of," said Mama, "is that if you don't stop this silly teasing, *I may lose my temper!*"

The cubs quickly finished their dinners and hurried off to do their homework.

59

Chapter 9
Where There's Smoke, There's Fire

The next afternoon, Brother, Sister, and Cousin Fred rode a special bus out to Miss Mamie's Riding Academy. So many cubs from Bear Country School were taking riding lessons this spring that Gus had hired a school bus for after-school lessons.

As the bus neared the academy, Brother told Fred, "Now remember: you pretend that you want to sign up for lessons. And after Gus shows you to the office, you slip out and go sniffing around for clues."

Fred didn't answer. He was sniffing at the air through the open window.

"I get it," said Brother. "*Sniffing for clues.*

Very funny. But all you'll get from here is a whiff of horses."

"Not horses," said Fred. He was still sniffing. "Smoke. And not burning leaves' smoke. *Wood* smoke."

"Hey, he's right," said Sister, who was sitting behind them. "Maybe it's a forest fire!"

"In a swamp?" said Brother.

Just then the bus turned into the academy driveway. There was a big red fire engine parked beside the office. It looked as if the firefighters were getting ready to leave. In front of the office stood Miss Mamie, Gus, and Fire Chief Barnes. When the bus came to a stop, the cubs piled out and crowded around the three grownups.

"It started in the stable fuse box," Chief Barnes was saying. "Lucky we got to it before it could do much damage. Gus, you'd better call an expert the next time you want to do more than change a fuse in that thing."

"I didn't touch that fuse box," Gus protested.

"Sorry, Gus," said the chief. "Knowing you're a handybear, I figured you must have—"

"I *swear* I didn't," said Gus.

"All right, all right," said the chief. "Don't get yourself in an uproar." He turned to

Miss Mamie and said, "My inspection turned up a dozen more fire hazards, ma'am." He looked down at his notepad. "Bales of rotting hay stacked in the stables, a pile of oily rags in a corner of the toolshed, an unsafe extension cord attached to the hot plate in the office, an exposed wire dangling from the back of the loudspeaker in the riding arena..."

As Chief Barnes read on, Miss Mamie's face sagged. When he had finished, she shook her head and said, "I can't understand it, Chief. I don't remember ever putting an extension cord on that hot plate."

"And I never piled oily rags in the toolshed," said Gus. "And when hay gets too old, I throw it out—pronto!"

"Anyone else work here?" asked the chief.

"Just my teenage assistants," said Miss Mamie. "But they only work with the horses."

"Wish I could figure it all out for you, Miss Mamie," said Chief Barnes. "But I've got to get back to the fire station. In the meantime, I'm going to issue you an official order to correct these problems. After seven days, I'll come back to inspect the place again. If the problems haven't been corrected by then, I'll have to shut the place down. Sorry, Miss Mamie. Just doin' my job."

Miss Mamie nodded. She was staring off into space again, as if her thoughts were a million miles away.

When Chief Barnes and the firefighters had gone, Miss Mamie looked around at her students and said, "I'm afraid I have to cancel today's lesson."

"No, Miss Mamie!" everyone cried. They all loved riding lessons. Even Brother was disappointed. Since his fall it had taken him a couple of lessons to get used to his horse, but he was already beginning to enjoy riding.

"And not just today's lesson," added Miss Mamie. "All lessons are canceled until these fire hazards are taken care of."

"But why?" asked Brother. "Chief Barnes gave you a whole week."

"As long as there's even *one* fire hazard at my academy, the place isn't safe enough for lessons. I may be a businessbear, but I won't gamble with the safety of cubs. Even if I end up losing this place." She shook her head sadly. "It's looking more and more like the darn thing is jinxed anyway."

With that, Miss Mamie limped off toward the stables. She left Gus and the cubs

standing in the driveway staring at each other.

"Will she be okay, Gus?" asked Sister. "She looks really upset."

"We'll just leave her be for a while," said Gus. "She'll come around. Meanwhile, we need to get an application form from the office for Cousin Fred."

"Oh, never mind—" Fred started to say.

"Shhh," whispered Brother. "Let's go with him. It'll give us a chance to ask some questions."

As the other cubs boarded the bus, Gus walked with Brother and Fred to the office.

"Do you still think the place might be haunted, Gus?" Brother asked.

"Naw," said Gus. "I thought it over. And I just don't believe in jinxes, ghosts, hauntings, or nothin' like that. Forbidden Bog may be a spooky place with a spooky legend, but this is somethin' else."

"Like what?" asked Fred.

They entered the office, and Gus handed Fred an application form.

"Like *sabotage*," said Gus.

"What?" said Brother.

" 'Sabotage,' " said Fred. "The deliberate undermining of a project or cause."

"Do you mean someone's doing it on purpose?" asked Brother.

"You bet I do," said Gus.

"But who?"

"I don't know," said Gus. "But whoever it is, they're being real careful about it. I've been over all the trouble spots with a fine-tooth comb. Didn't find a speck of evidence."

They headed back to the waiting bus.

"If lessons are canceled for a whole week," said Brother, "then how will Miss

Mamie pay the mortgage?"

"That's another question I don't have the answer to," said Gus. "I'm afraid Miss Mamie's Riding Academy is beginning to look like a lost cause."

Later, on the way home, Brother looked off into the spooky darkness of Forbidden Bog and shook his head. "Grizzlock Holmes didn't believe in jinxes," he told Cousin Fred. "And neither do I. Gus is right. Someone is causing these so-called accidents."

"But who?" asked Fred.

Brother shrugged. "Grizzlock Holmes would know how to find out. But not me. So far I'm clueless."

"If we can't figure out who it is, Miss Mamie is going to lose the academy," said Fred.

"I'm afraid so," said Brother. He was deep in thought. "Unless there's some way we could help her raise the money for that mortgage payment…"

Chapter 10
Cubs to the Rescue

All afternoon Brother thought about how to help Miss Mamie. He thought about it all evening. And he thought about it all the next morning in Teacher Bob's class.

By lunchtime he had come up with an idea. First he talked with Sister, Fred, Babs, and Queenie. Then they talked with all the other riding students. They decided to form a committee called Friends of Miss Mamie. They would meet later that evening at the Burger Bear to go over a plan of action.

At the Burger Bear, the Friends of Miss Mamie decided on three things. First, they would all pitch in to clean up Miss Mamie's place so that Fire Chief Barnes could declare it safe. Second, they would organize a big event to raise enough money for Miss

THE FRIENDS OF MISS MAMIE
PRESENT
THE GREATEST
HORSE SHOW
ON EARTH

PRIZES   GAMES   SHOWS   EVENTS

Mamie's late mortgage payment. And third, they would get their parents to help Miss Mamie become a better businessbear so that she would never again be late with a mortgage payment.

For the fund-raising event, the cubs decided to put on a big outdoor horse show and fair. Over the next few days, the Friends of Miss Mamie worked very hard to organize the big show. First they drew up some plans and made some phone calls. Soon a really great show was taking shape. There would be exhibition riding, jumping, and stunts by Miss Mamie's teenage assistants. The students themselves would show off their riding skills. There would be booths for face-painting, weight-guessing, palm-reading, and a ring toss game. Even Ralph Ripoff would be there to fool bears with his famous shell game. (But this time it would be for a good cause!) The name of the show would be "The Greatest Horse Show on Earth."

Harry "Wheels" McGill printed up the announcement posters for the big show on his computer. And the Friends of Miss Mamie posted them all over town. Meanwhile, Gus persuaded Miss Mamie to let the cubs clean up the academy. He also got permission from Bear Country School to have a school bus take them out to the academy on a Sunday afternoon for the big clean-up.

The clean-up was hard work. But it went smoothly. Brother and Fred took the oily rags out of the toolshed and burned them. Queenie's father hauled away the rotting hay in his pickup truck. Babs, Queenie, Sister, and Lizzy put new fire-resistant tiles on the office roof.

By dusk the Friends of Miss Mamie were all very tired. But they were also very proud of themselves.

Chapter 11
A Visitor from the Bog

After the clean-up, the cubs crowded into the office, where Miss Mamie made hot chocolate for everyone. They sat on the floor and drank from their mugs as night fell.

"I can't thank you cubs enough," said Miss Mamie. She looked over at Gus and chuckled. "Gus and I were beginning to think this place was jinxed. You cubs sure put that idea to rest. No school or business could be jinxed and have such a loyal bunch of friends at the same time."

"And don't you worry about that mortgage payment, Miss Mamie," said Brother Bear. "Our show will raise enough money to pay last month's *and* this month's mortgage!"

"That would be mighty nice," said Miss Mamie. "Well, the bus is waiting, and I hear a storm brewing out there. You cubs better get on home."

The cubs put their empty mugs on Miss Mamie's desk and started for the door. Just then they heard a faint howling from the

H-H-H-H-❀-❀-❀-❀-❀

WHAT WAS THAT?

JUST THE WIND WHISTLING THROUGH THOSE OLD TWISTED BOG TREES.

direction of Forbidden Bog. Sister stopped in her tracks. "What was that?" she said.

Brother was right behind her. "Just the wind whistling through those old twisted bog trees," he said.

W-W-W-L-L-L-L

"But it's getting louder," said Miss Mamie. She went to the window, and looked out. "Nothing there," she said. "No. Wait. There's something moving out there in the bog."

Gus hurried to the door and threw it open. The cubs crowded around him and stared wide-eyed into the darkness. There it was! A glowing form moved through the darkened bog, flickering as it passed behind trees and vines.

As Miss Mamie, Gus, and the cubs watched, the form suddenly burst from the bog and came into full view. It was a ghostly, glowing bear riding a ghostly, glowing horse! And it was galloping right toward them!

"Good heavens!" cried Miss Mamie. "Quick, Gus, shut that door!"

Gus slammed and bolted the door. The cubs huddled in the middle of the room.

All trembled in terror as the howling got louder and louder. It passed so close to the office that it sent shivers down their spines. Then it moved away in the direction of the bog, growing fainter and fainter until it was gone.

For a time no one said a word. At last

Miss Mamie broke the spooky silence.

"So it's true!" she gasped. "The old legend is true! The Galloping Ghost of Forbidden Bog is real!"

"But...but...," Gus stammered. No matter how hard he tried, he couldn't get another word out.

The cubs were all so badly shaken that they couldn't speak at all.

"That does it!" said Miss Mamie. "This place isn't just jinxed. It's haunted, too! I'm closing it down. The big show is canceled. All riding lessons are canceled."

"For how long?" asked Gus.

"Until further notice."

"But what about your mortgage payment?" asked Brother.

"It'll just have to go unpaid," said Miss Mamie.

"But you'll lose the academy," said Cousin Fred.

"So be it," said Miss Mamie. "I'm not going to fool around with the supernatural. No, sir!"

Brother wanted to argue with Miss Mamie. But he didn't even try. He was so confused. A glowing ghost on a glowing horse—he had seen them with his own eyes! And they had looked every bit as real as anything he had ever seen.

Miss Mamie swung the door open and moved toward the bus. "It's starting to rain, cubs," she said. "Let's get you on the bus." Bessie, the driver, was staring wide eyed into the bog. Miss Mamie had to bang on

the door to get Bessie to open it. The cubs were so shaken up that Gus had to lead them to the bus.

As the cubs climbed onto the bus, Miss Mamie thanked each one of them. Brother was last in line to get on. Miss Mamie shook his hand and gave him a special thanks for organizing Friends of Miss Mamie.

"I don't know what to say, Miss Mamie," said Brother. "I wish this all could have turned out different."

"Me, too," said Miss Mamie. "I guess maybe I should have taken that offer."

"Offer?" said Brother.

"Yes," said Miss Mamie. "It was a real generous one, too. A couple of months ago, a group of strangers from Big Bear City offered to buy the academy. I turned them down, of course. Told them the academy was my life and wasn't for sale at any price."

"Maybe you could still sell it to them," said Brother.

"After what just happened?" said Miss Mamie. "Word about the Galloping Ghost showing up here will spread like wildfire. By noon tomorrow there won't be a buyer in all of Bear Country who would touch this place with a ten-*mile* pole."

"I guess you're right," said Brother. "But maybe you could find someone who doesn't believe in ghosts—"

"I didn't think *I* believed in ghosts," said Miss Mamie. "But after what I saw tonight, well...I don't know what to believe." A bolt of lightning split the sky. It was followed by a loud clap of thunder and a gust of rain. "Wow! That was close. Into the bus with you."

Chapter 12
To Catch a Ghost

Forbidden Bog looked spookier than ever as the school bus passed it in the night. The cubs watched for signs of the Galloping Ghost. But the bog was as black as coal.

Brother Bear wondered if the ghost had returned to his quicksand grave. But had it really been a ghost? Brother tried to imagine what Grizzlock Holmes would say. He could hear the great bear detective's voice in his mind: "I say, Bearson, do you really believe that only ghosts glow in the dark?"

Just then Brother remembered what Miss Mamie had told him as he was about to board the bus. *Aha!* he thought. I've got it! "Stop the bus!" he cried.

Bessie looked back in surprise. "What?"

"Turn around and go back to the academy!" said Brother. "I have something *very important* to tell Miss Mamie!"

Great flashes of lightning again split the sky as the bus turned around on the narrow road. By the time they reached the academy, rain was pouring down. The dirt driveway was quickly turning to mud. Before the cubs could reach the door, Miss Mamie opened it and limped down the steps.

"What is it, cubs?" she said.

"Miss Mamie!" shouted Brother over the rumble of thunder. "I think I know what's going on around here!"

"You *do*?" said Miss Mamie. "Come out of the rain and tell me about it."

But just then the weird howling started again.

"Look!" cried Miss Mamie. "The Galloping Ghost! He's coming back!"

The cubs turned in time to see the glowing horse and rider jump the fence at the edge of the bog and come galloping straight at them. The cubs started to run for the office. But Brother shouted, "Wait! Stand your ground."

Which is just what he did. He stood there in the pouring rain, facing the ghostly rider and its steed as they came closer and closer.

Then the strangest thing of all happened.

WAIT! STAND YOUR GROUND!

As the Galloping Ghost raced toward Brother and his friends, the glow of his ghostly horse began to fade. *The horse was disappearing before their very eyes!*

The cubs wanted to turn and run. But all

of a sudden Brother ran straight toward the ghost, shouting, "After him, gang! Get him!"

When the cubs saw Brother's bravery, they got back their courage and followed him. But before they could reach the ghost, it turned and galloped back toward Forbidden Bog.

By now the ghost's horse was almost

invisible. Heading for the fence, the glowing ghost bounced along as if in mid-air. With a tremendous leap, the horse jumped the fence and escaped into the bog. But the glowing ghost wasn't so lucky. He lost his balance in mid-leap and fell right into the thornbushes that covered the fence.

"Come on, gang!" yelled Brother. "He's trapped!"

The cubs reached the fence. But because the thornbushes were so dense they didn't try to grab the ghost. The ghost struggled to free himself from the thorns. He was still glowing, but up close he didn't look much like a ghost anymore. Instead, he looked a lot like a bear wearing a glowing sheet.

Gus and Miss Mamie were not far behind.

"Get that sheet off the varmint!" barked Miss Mamie.

"With pleasure," said Gus. He poked the

branch into the thornbush and lifted up the glowing sheet.

"Well, I'll be!" said Miss Mamie. "Look who it is!"

"His initials are B. B. all right," said Gus. "But he isn't Billy Beechtree. He's Billy *Bogg*!"

The youngest Bogg brother stopped struggling long enough to scowl at Gus, Miss Mamie, and the cubs.

"I thought the Bogg brothers were still in jail on their drug conviction," said Cousin Fred.

"They must have gotten out," said Miss Mamie.

"I'll go call the police," said Gus.

"Let me do it," said Babs Bruno. "After all, the chief is my dad." She headed for the office at a run.

Just then Billy Bogg's horse came walking out of the bog. It was looking for its master. Its glow was completely gone. Miss Mamie took hold of the animal's reins and calmed it down.

Cousin Fred held up the glowing sheet. "Hey," he said. "This sheet must have been dipped in chemicals that glow. I'll bet the horse was painted with them, and they got washed off by the rain."

"What an awful thing to do to a horse!" said Miss Mamie. She turned on Billy Bogg with fire in her eyes. "What in tarnation are you up to, mister!" she snapped.

"Nothin' that concerns the likes of *you*,"

growled Billy Bogg. "There's no law against practicing for Halloween, is there?"

Miss Mamie roared with laughter. " 'Practicing for Halloween,' he says! Six months early!"

Billy Bogg yanked at the thorns that still held him fast. "I need a lot of practice," he grumbled.

"Well, there may not be a law against riding around in a glowing sheet," said Miss Mamie. "But there *are* laws against trespassing on private property and mistreating animals. And you can bet your muddy boots I'll press charges."

Just then the police chief's car, its blue and red lights flashing, came speeding up the academy driveway. Chief Bruno and Officer Marguerite got out and hurried over to the group of bears.

"Well, well," said Chief Bruno when he saw Billy Bogg. "Out of jail for two short weeks and already in trouble again." He grabbed Billy Bogg's arms and hauled him out of the thornbush. "You're headed downtown for questioning, Billy. Cuff him, Officer Marguerite."

As Officer Marguerite led the handcuffed Bogg brother to the chief's car, Miss Mamie explained to Chief Bruno what had happened that evening.

"And that's not all, Chief," said Brother when she had finished. "I think you'll find that he and his brothers are behind all these strange accidents and fire hazards at the academy."

"Why would the Bogg brothers want to hurt Miss Mamie's business?" asked the chief.

"For money," said Brother. "Someone paid them to do it. And I think I know who." He smiled proudly.

"Well, out with it," said Miss Mamie.

"It's whoever bought Miss Mamie's mortgage from Great Grizzly National Bank," replied Brother. "And I'll bet they're the very same bears who wanted to buy the academy two months ago."

"Buy the academy?" said Gus with surprise. "You never told me about that, Miss Mamie."

"Didn't think it was important," said Miss Mamie. "I just happened to mention it to Brother when he was getting on the bus tonight to go home. It's a good thing I did."

"Hmm," said Gus, stroking his chin. "I think I get the picture. Miss Mamie wouldn't sell to those real-estate folks, so they bought her mortgage from the bank and tried to ruin her business so they could foreclose."

"Exactly," said Brother. "They hired the Bogg brothers to sabotage the academy—to do things like leave the stable window open and the hose running all night, to loosen the bolts in the railing and mess with the fuse box. The mortgage owners wanted to get the academy closed down so Miss Mamie couldn't catch up on her mortgage pay-

SOMEONE PAID THEM TO DO IT. AND I THINK I KNOW WHO.

WELL, OUT WITH IT.

ments. Then they would take over the academy. For a while it looked as if their scheme were working. But then we formed Friends of Miss Mamie and planned the big horse show to raise money. So they tried to get us to cancel the show by making us think the academy was haunted. And it almost worked."

"Sounds like a mighty good theory," said Chief Bruno. "I'll check it out and let you all know what happens. But first, I think I'll snoop around a little in the bog. You know those Bogg brothers—wherever there's one, the others can't be far behind."

The chief aimed his flashlight at a gap in the fence. As he walked toward it he looked back over his shoulder and said, "And good luck with your big show."

"Thanks, Chief," the cubs said all at once. There were big grins all around.

Chapter 13
The Show Must Go On

Sure enough, Chief Bruno caught Bart and Bert Bogg trying to drive out of Forbidden Bog in a horse van. He questioned all three Bogg brothers at the police station. As it turned out, Brother was exactly right about what had happened.

The Bogg brothers had been hired by a group of real-estate developers from Big Bear City to sabotage Miss Mamie's Riding Academy. This group wanted to tear down the academy and build a huge shopping mall in its place. They were the same bears,

THE GREATEST HORSE
SHOW ON EARTH

of course, who owned Miss Mamie's mortgage and who had earlier tried to buy the
academy from her. Chief Bruno phoned the
Big Bear City police, who arrested them.

Miss Mamie's mortgage was taken over
again by Great Grizzly National Bank. That
made her very happy. But she was still

behind on her payments. She wanted to put an end to that, once and for all.

Soon the day of the big show arrived. The Greatest Horse Show on Earth was open for business! Bears from all over Bear Country crowded onto the grounds of Miss Mamie's Riding Academy. A huge riding ring had been set up in the middle of the front lawn. Miss Mamie's assistants, then her students, performed for the crowd. And even though they were the newest students, Brother and Sister did themselves proud. Mama and Papa Bear beamed as they watched.

The big show was such a success that enough money was raised for the late mortgage payment—just from the sale of admission tickets alone. But there was much more to see than just the horse show.

Around the riding ring were booths of all kinds: ring tosses, weight-guessers, fortune-tellers. The longest line of all was at Ralph Ripoff's shell game. From dawn to dusk, Ralph's booming voice rang out over the

crowd: "Step right up, ladies and gents! Try your luck! The hand is quicker than the eye! Now you see it, now you don't!" By closing time, Ralph had raised enough money all by himself to pay another month of Miss Mamie's mortgage.

But the biggest attraction of all was one that no one had planned. It was Miss Mamie herself. With a big friendly smile, the grand old lady went from bear to bear, thanking one and all for their support. And the amazing thing was that she wasn't limping. That's because she was riding the beautiful Flash!

Miss Mamie was so glad to keep her riding academy that for the first time in nine long years, she had found the courage to get back in the saddle.

Stan and Jan Berenstain began writing and illustrating books for children in the early 1960s, when their two young sons were beginning to read. That marked the start of the best-selling Berenstain Bears series. Now, with more than 95 books in print, videos, television shows, and even Berenstain Bears attractions at major amusement parks, it's hard to tell where the Bears end and the Berenstains begin!

Stan and Jan make their home in Bucks County, Pennsylvania, near their sons—Leo, a writer, and Michael, an illustrator—who are helping them with Big Chapter Books stories and pictures. They plan on writing and illustrating many more books for children, especially for their four grandchildren, who keep them well in touch with the kids of today.